MONTY
Cat of Ave Maria

By
Patricia Sette

For my daughter, Mariana, the "Mary Ann" of this story.

Publishers Cataloging-in-Publication Data
Sette, Patricia
Monty, Cat of Ave Maria / Patricia Sette: illustrated by Tom Cardamone
Summary: When Monty the cat is prevented from peeking inside the church building in his town, he sneaks in on his own one night and meets a "king."
montyavemaria@gmail.com

ISBN 978-0-615-22776-4
[1. Cats – Juvenile fiction. 2. Catholic Church – Juvenile fiction 3. Ave Maria town – Juvenile fiction]
I. Cardamone, Tom, ill. II. Title

Designed by TCA Graphics, Naples, FL.
Email address: tomsart4526@aol.com

For personal, bulk or retail orders of this book, please email montyavemaria@gmail.com.

It was early in the morning in the town of Ave Maria, Florida. Monty the cat looked down from the window sill of the apartment where he lived to the town below. He waited.

He waited as he watched Mrs. Lopez and Mr. Lopez eat their muffins at a table near the coffee shop. He waited while he saw Sister Joan Mary walk along the brick path to teach the children at the school.

3

And he waited while Monica, John and Mary Ellen rode their bikes over the bridge, pedaling as fast as they could. "Hurry, we're almost late for class!" John cried.
They were almost late every morning.

Then, Mary Ann came into the room with Monty's harness and leash the way she did every morning. "Time for our walk," she told him.

Monty purred a great rumbling purr as Mary Ann put his harness on him. This is what he had been waiting for.

Monty felt the warmth of the brick sidewalk under his paws.

He felt the coolness on his back when they passed under the shade of a palm tree. He lifted his tail high.

He was Monty – cat of Ave Maria.

"Good morning, Monty," said Mrs. Harper as she walked by.

"It's Monty!" said the twins Susan and Steven, as Monty strolled past them with his tail in the air.

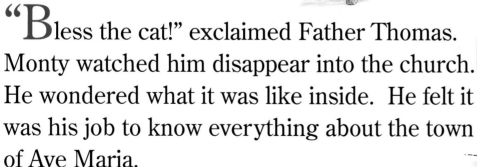

"Bless the cat!" exclaimed Father Thomas. Monty watched him disappear into the church. He wondered what it was like inside. He felt it was his job to know everything about the town of Ave Maria.

7

He did know what the other buildings in Ave Maria looked like inside.

He knew all about the toy store, because he
always stopped in to say hello to Mrs. Allan,
the lady who owned the shop.

"Have a cat treat," she would say.

He also knew all about Mr. Dix's coffee shop, because Mary Ann would tuck him under her arm and bring him in when she went for her morning coffee.

"Have some bagel," Mr. Dix would say, giving Monty a small piece.

There wasn't any food waiting for Monty in Mr. Melvin's bike shop, but there was something even better – a large white bird named King, with a fine crown of yellow feathers on his head.

Bink-boink! Up Monty jumped for a closer look. His tail twitched. King fluttered and squawked. But Mr. Melvin just said, "Aw, King, stop your fussing. He can't get you in that cage." And then Mr. Melvin made the same joke he made every time Monty visited.

"You know, even a cat may look at a king."

Neither Monty nor King had the faintest idea what Mr. Melvin was talking about.

But when Monty would try to peek through the large doors leading inside the church that stood in the middle of the town, Mary Ann would just pull him back gently and laugh.

"You're pretty silly, Monty," she would say. "A cat can't go to church."

Sometimes at night, Monty would hop on the wall of his balcony and stare at the church. He would look very still. But he wouldn't feel still inside one bit. He, Monty, cat of Ave Maria, had never had even one peek inside the town's most beautiful building.

It was very annoying.

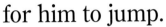Monty would imagine jumping down to the slanty roof below him to go over to the church and peek inside. But whenever he looked at the slanty roof in the moonlight, it always seemed too far down for him to jump.

14

But this night, for the first time, he saw that the slanty roof was *not* too far.

So he jumped down ...

He had not planned on sliding ...

And he did not have a chance to decide if he wanted to drop down to the balcony below. He just did.

He found himself on Mrs. Harper's balcony in the middle of three potted plants. Monty began pouncing among the little bushes. He even ate one of the leaves so he would know all about them. It was his job to know about everything in Ave Maria.

When he was all finished finding out about the plants, he jumped down to the sidewalk below.

Bink-boink. In a few easy hops, Monty reached the church door.

Inside, it was very dark. But in the front, Monty saw a bright light.
He walked toward it with his tail held high. There was so much to look
at on the right and on the left. He even looked under the benches to
see if there might be a mouse, but he couldn't find one.

So, he gazed up to the tall, tall ceiling. He could not see the top.

When he almost reached the front, Monty was surprised to see Mrs. Harper sitting there. He had thought everyone in Ave Maria was sleeping. And then Monty saw Mrs. Harper *was* sleeping, with her prayer book in her lap.

Monty found himself gazing at a long table. On the table seemed to be something shining and gold, with something white gleaming in the center. He found for the first time in his life, he did not want to jump, bink-boink, to see better. He simply looked and …

... OH!

And he sat there, on top of the pew right next to Mrs. Harper.

He looked very still...

... and he felt very still.

After a long, long time, Monty felt gentle arms lifting him up. "Ah, bless the cat," Father Thomas was saying softly as the morning light began to stream through the windows. "So it is true – even a cat may look at a King."

Mrs. Harper opened her eyes, startled.
"Oh, dear, Father Thomas. I must have fallen asleep
when it was my turn to keep watch in prayer."

"It is all right," said Father Thomas.
"It seems that someone else was called to
do the watching for you."

Later that morning, Monty went for his walk again with Mary Ann.
He held his tail higher than ever before. He knew – or almost knew –
everything in the town around him. After all, he was

Monty – cat of Ave Maria.